# How
# W A R
## Changed Rondo

Written and illustrated by
## Romana Romanyshyn
## Andriy Lesiv

Translated from Ukrainian by
## Oksana Lushchevska

*Enchanted Lion Books*
NEW YORK

The town of Rondo was like no other. There, the air was uncommonly clear, as if spun from pure light. The town's residents were unusual, too. They grew flowers, tended the parks and gardens, and built distinctive houses. They also spoke to birds and plants, painted pictures, sang, and wrote poetry. Everyone liked living in Rondo. But the three friends Danko, Fabian, and Zirka loved Rondo best of all, and were known throughout the town.

Danko

Fabian

Zirka

RONDO

Danko had a thin, transparent body that glowed like a lantern. His heart shone brightest. He often rode his bicycle through the town, humming melodies from his favorite movies. Inside his bicycle basket, he kept a thick atlas with old engravings of plants, flowers, and trees.

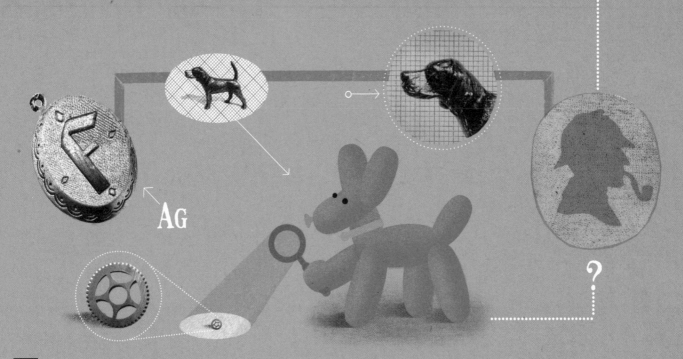

Fabian, who came from a long line of treasure hunters, had a good nose and sharp eyes. He was so light that even the slightest breeze would have lifted him up and carried him away were it not for his silver medallion, engraved with the letter "F". The medallion was large and heavy, but Fabian never took it off. It kept him firmly planted on the ground.

Zirka could fly. She soared high in the sky and could even perform complex aerobatics. In the air, she flapped her paper wings; back on earth, she covered them with notes and sketches of her journeys. More than anything, she loved to travel.

R ondo was famous for its flowers. The pride of the town was a large greenhouse located on the main square. It housed a collection of rare flowers and plants from the farthest corners of the earth. But the most wonderful thing of all was that all of the flowers could sing.

# Greenhouse

There were frequent concerts in the greenhouse. The vocal performances of the town's anthem—Mozart's *Rondo alla Turca*—were the biggest draw. Visitors from far and wide came for the incredible show. And the chorus of flowers also sang every morning at dawn, as each flower reverently raised its face to the sun.

PAPAVER RHOEAS

TAGETES PATULA

D anko went to the greenhouse every day before dawn. He loved to start his day singing with the flowers. No one knew how to care for them like he did. He made sure they were content and had plenty of water and light. He also diligently studied their entries in his atlas—including their long Latin names—because he wanted to understand what each flower needed the most.

After, Danko usually met Fabian at the café around the corner, where they would discuss the latest news. From there, they would go to Zirka's, even though they never knew if she would be home, since she often went on long journeys and was gone for days at a time.

In Rondo, it was a day like any other day. People were rushing about, doing their usual business. Danko was on his way to meet his friends. Zirka had just returned from a trip and had lots of new stories and drawings. The sun was shining, and the flowers and birds were singing. Everything seemed normal, until all went completely still.

And a whisper arose …

# WAR

is coming to Rondo

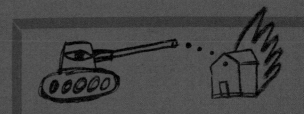

Nobody knew what War was. It seemed to come from nowhere. It was black and scary. It rumbled and roared. It crept slowly toward Rondo, bringing destruction, turmoil, and dense darkness. Everything it touched disappeared into nothingness. Most frightening of all were the black flowers and the dry, spiked weeds War planted in its wake. Mute and scentless, these flowers erupted from the earth, forming dense thickets that blotted out the sun. Without light, the delicate and defenseless flowers of Rondo started to weaken and fade, sapped of the strength they needed to raise their faces to the sky. Saddest of all, they stopped singing.

Danko, Fabian, and Zirka, always gentle, yet brave, resisted War and its darkness. At first, they tried talking to it and asked it to go away. But War simply ignored them and marched stubbornly on, with its terrible clicking and hissing machines, which hurled sharp stones and spit fire.

One of the stones hit Danko in the chest, over his heart, causing cracks that radiated outward. Fiery sparks rained down on Zirka, burning the edges of her wings. As for Fabian, a black, thorny flower erupted right in front of him and pierced his leg.

War touched everyone.

WORLD
IN A TOTAL
WAR

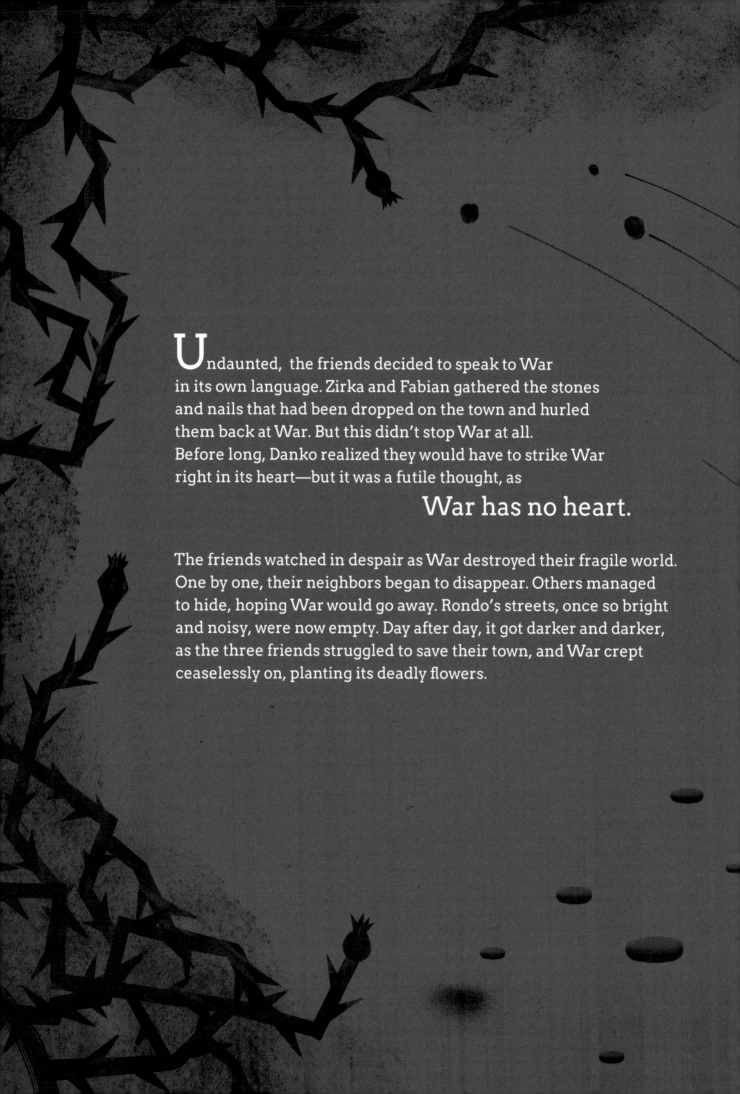

Undaunted, the friends decided to speak to War in its own language. Zirka and Fabian gathered the stones and nails that had been dropped on the town and hurled them back at War. But this didn't stop War at all. Before long, Danko realized they would have to strike War right in its heart—but it was a futile thought, as

### War has no heart.

The friends watched in despair as War destroyed their fragile world. One by one, their neighbors began to disappear. Others managed to hide, hoping War would go away. Rondo's streets, once so bright and noisy, were now empty. Day after day, it got darker and darker, as the three friends struggled to save their town, and War crept ceaselessly on, planting its deadly flowers.

Danko continued to go to the greenhouse, except now he had to sneak in. Smog had darkened its windows, and the few remaining flowers hung wilted and silent in a far corner. One day, when the darkness in town was so dense that it was nearly impossible to see, Danko tried to revive the flowers by shining his small bicycle light on them. Anchoring his bicycle to the floor, he aimed the light at the plants and pedaled. As soon as the beam of light reached them, they began to throb, and their dim hues brightened. Danko pedaled faster and faster, and the light became brighter and brighter.

Then, Danko started to sing the town's anthem, which hadn't been heard in Rondo for a long time. After the first verse, one flower raised its head and began to sing along. Then a second flower joined in, and a third. Soon, a dozen flowers were singing.

It was then that Danko lost hold of the handlebars and the beam of light hit War, which had just entered a neighboring street. When it did, an incredible thing happened: War went completely still. For an instant, its harsh sounds ceased, and all that could be heard was the singing of the flowers.

Danko saw it all. War was scared, because even with its great force, it couldn't resist the singing of the flowers. For the truth is that even the smallest ray of light will begin to disperse the darkness. Now the friends understood: to stop War, they would have to build a huge light machine to destroy its darkness and save the singing flowers.

The three friends got to work immediately. Others joined in. Soon, the center of town looked like a busy anthill, with each doing their best and everyone united in common cause.

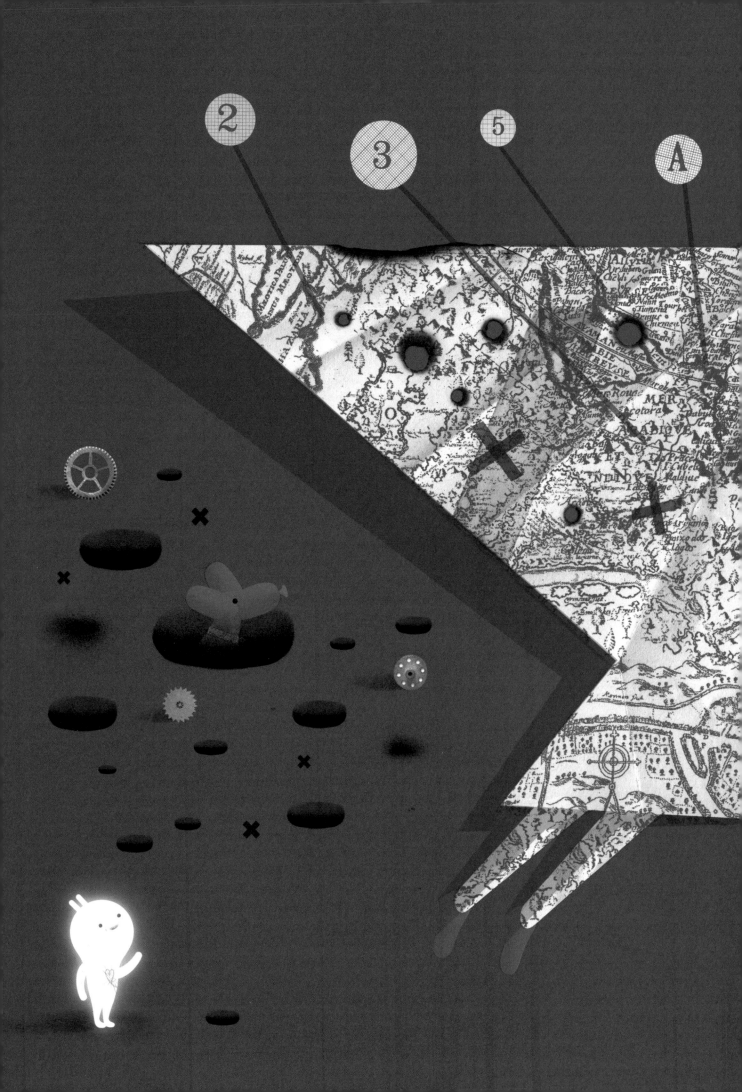

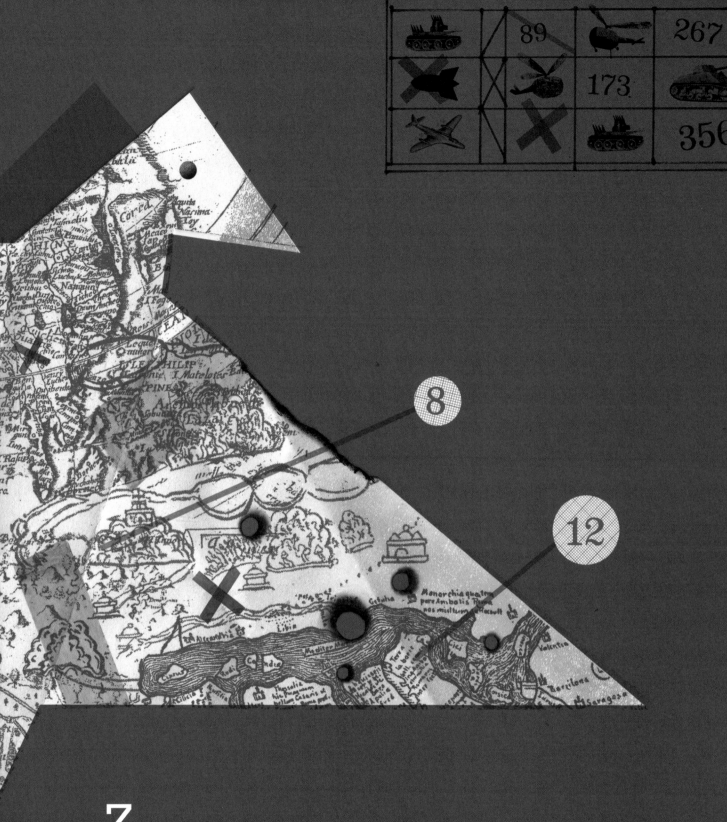

| | | | 267 |
|---|---|---|---|
| | | 173 | |
| | | | 356 |

8

12

**Z**irka gathered information, drawing maps of where War was and recording important data on her wings. Fabian gathered parts for the light machine, and Danko oversaw the machine's construction, guided by an old book on mechanics that he had found.

When the machine was finished, they each took up their station, ready to act in unison. Hundreds of pedals and thousands of gears started to spin simultaneously, bringing the machine to life. Bright light streamed through the streets as Danko, Fabian, Zirka, the townspeople, and the flowers began to sing.

War froze, then slowly started to dissolve in the light. The brighter the light became and the stronger the singing, the faster War and its darkness dissipated, along with its prickly black flowers.

The whole town sang until every black flower had disappeared and the darkness had dissolved completely.

VICTORY!

Soon, poppies began to spring up where the black flowers had been. Once upon a time, before War had come to Rondo, the poppies had been pink, yellow, violet, purple, and white. Now, all of the poppies were red.

The residents of Rondo slowly rebuilt the greenhouse and the rest of their town. Just as before, the flowers grew and sang each morning.

But not everything in Rondo could be fully repaired.
Danko's transparent body is still cracked around his heart;
the edges of Zirka's wings are scarred from being burnt;
and Fabian now limps from his wound.

Their neighbors also bear scars. Each has sorrowful memories of War,
and how it changed Rondo forever.

To this day, red poppies grow throughout the town.*

---

* The red poppy is the international symbol of remembrance, commemorating those who died
  fighting wars. It came into use in 1914, with World War I.

**UKRAINIAN**
**//IIIBOOK**
**INSTITUTE**

This book has been published with the support
of the Translate Ukraine Translation Program
*Ця книга видана за підтримки програми*
*перекладів Translate Ukraine*

www.enchantedlion.com

First English-language edition published in 2021 by Enchanted Lion Books
248 Creamer Street, Studio 4, Brooklyn, NY 11231
Originally published in 2015 under the title *Війна, що змінила Рондо*
by Vydavnytstvo Staroho Leva (The Old Lion Publishing House), Lviv, Ukraine
Text and illustrations © 2015 by Romana Romanyshyn and Andriy Lesiv
English-language translation copyright © 2021 by Oksana Lushchevska
Editors, English-language text: Claudia Zoe Bedrick and Lawrence Kim
All rights reserved under International and Pan-American Copyright Conventions
A CIP is on record with the Library of Congress
ISBN 978-1-59270-367-8
Printed in Italy by Società Editoriale Grafiche AZ
First Printing